Copyright text and illustration © Elmo en de kleine zeehond by Rick de Haas.
Amsterdam, 2009 Uitgeverij Leopold B.V.
English text copyright © 2012 by North-South Books Inc., New York 10017.
All rights reserved.
No part of this book may be reproduced or utilized in any form or by any means, electronic
or mechanical, including photo-copying, recording, or any information storage and retrieval
system, without permission in writing from the publisher.

First published in the United States, Great Britain, Canada, Australia, and New Zealand in 2012
by North-South Books, Inc., an imprint of NordSüd Verlag AG, CH-8005 Zürich, Switzerland.

Designed by Pamela Darcy.
Distributed in the United States by North-South Books Inc., New York 10017.
Library of Congress Cataloging-in-Publication Data is available.
ISBN: 978-0-7358-4061-4 (trade edition)
1 3 5 7 9 · 10 8 6 4 2
Printed in Germany by Grafisches Centrum Cuno GmbH & Co. KG, 39240 Calbe, November 2011.
www.northsouth.com

FSC
www.fsc.org
MIX
Paper from
responsible sources
FSC® C043106

Rick de Haas

Peter
and the
Seal

NorthSouth
New York / London

It was a warm day.

Peter was hiding out in the shade.

"Why don't you go boating," said Grandma. "It must be cooler on the water."

What a good idea, thought Peter. "Come on, Leo!"

Peter and his dog ran to the jetty where Peter had anchored his little submarine.

"Be back in time for dinner!" called Grandma.

It was nice and cool on the water, and the sea was
perfectly calm.

"Pull your head in, Leo!" said Peter. "We're going to dive."

As peaceful as it was above the surface, it was busy
underwater. Little sardines, starfish, and all kinds
of animals Peter didn't even know by name lived there.

Above them the sun was shining on the water.

"Look!" said Peter. "There's a bird swimming above us. It's a gull!"

But when you're in a submarine, you also have to look where you're going—especially when the tide is out. *Woosh!*

With a soft scraping sound, the submarine ground to a halt.

"Oh, no!" said Peter. "We bumped into a sandbank."

When the water went down, Peter and Leo got out of the submarine. Peter tried to push the little boat.

"It's completely stuck," he said. "We'll have to stay here overnight. Tomorrow we can get away when the high tide comes in. But Grandma will be so worried!"

Together Peter and Leo explored the sandbank.
"We're not alone here," Peter said. "Look!"
There was a crab, a few mussels, and a ray's egg.

Nighttime came. The summer sky was clear and full
of stars. Peter took a sleeping bag out of the submarine.
  "Will you come sit with me, Leo?" he asked. "Look, a
shooting star. Quick, make a wish!"
  But Leo didn't make a wish. He was growling and looking
into the darkness.

Peter saw the light of the lighthouse in the distance.
Grandma must be having dinner now, he thought. And my
bed will be empty tonight.

Leo jumped down from the submarine onto the sand.

"What is it? What are you doing?" asked Peter.

Then he heard it too. There was a shuffling sound in the
water just beyond the light of the submarine.

"Maybe we should go to sleep now, Leo. It will be morning
soon and then we can go home."

Quickly they jumped into the submarine.
Peter closed the hatch.

"We won't open it till tomorrow morning," he said.

"Nothing can happen to us."

Inside the submarine Peter kept some food for emergencies: a roll of crackers and a bottle of lemonade.

"Would you like something to eat, Leo?" he asked.

But Leo didn't want a cracker. He pricked up his ears.

"You're so restless," said Peter. "I'm going to sleep now. Good night."

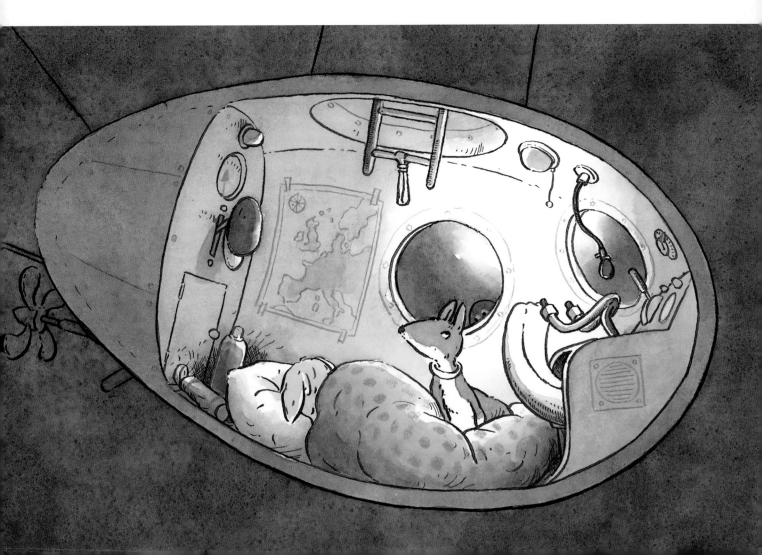

Suddenly the submarine moved. It tumbled over—first only
halfway and then, with a bang, completely on its side into
the wet sand.

Peter, Leo, and everything went flying around.

"What's this?" Peter called out. "We have to find out what happened."

He grabbed his flashlight and opened the hatch.

Peter shone his light outside the submarine. A crab walked
through the beam of light.

"Hey, you," Peter called out with a brave voice. "Did you
push us over?"

Suddenly, he heard the shuffling sound again. Leo started to
bark loudly. Peter shone his light behind the submarine.

Could there be a big submarine-toppling monster?

"Look!" said Peter. "A baby seal!
Are you all by yourself? Where is
your mother?"
   The little seal was squeaking softly.

Peter lifted him up and took him inside the submarine.

"Are you hungry?" he asked. "Would you like a cracker?"

Leo sniffed at the baby seal.

"Shhh!" Peter said softly. "He smells like fish, but we won't mention it because that wouldn't be polite."

The little seal wagged his tail and looked around with his big seal eyes.

"Come sleep here tonight," said Peter. "Good night."

Finally the sun started to rise. Peter and Leo worked hard. They dug a big hole behind the submarine. And they attached ropes to the side and then pulled hard. The baby seal helped too. A little bit.

The tide was coming in. The water was rising and rising. Then, with a soft sigh, the submarine was lifted up from the sand.

"Come with us!" Peter said to the baby seal. "I bet you're a good swimmer, but you're too small to stay behind on your own. Grandma will know what to do about you."

The engine started and Peter accelerated. Suddenly
he longed very much to see the lighthouse and Grandma.
Then he heard something above them.

"Hey, Gull!" he called. "Would you like a cracker?"

In less than fifteen minutes they saw the jetty.
It looked very crowded. Peter saw Grandma.
"Hello, we're back!" he called.

The baby seal also popped his head out. "Look!" said Peter. "There's someone waiting for you too. I told you that Grandma always has a solution for everything!"